THE GINGERBREAD MAN

And other stories
for 4-7 year olds

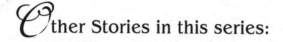

ℭontents continued

Contents

To all those parents, storytellers and teachers who keep the flame of stories alive in children's minds.

To Edmund - more stories for your golden box.

Introduction © 2008, Pie Corbett
2008 Scholastic Ltd
Illustrations © Harris Sofokleous/Sylvie Poggio
Designed using Adobe InDesign

Published by Scholastic Ltd
Villiers House
Clarendon Avenue
Leamington Spa
Warwickshire
CV32 5PR
www.scholastic.co.uk

Printed in the UK by CPI Bookmarque

1 2 3 4 5 6 7 8 9   8 9 0 1 2 3 4 5 6 7

British Library Cataloguing-in-Publication Data
A catalogue record for this book is available from the British Library.

ISBN 978-1407-10064-7

Acknowledgements

Every effort has been made to trace copyright holders for the works reproduced in this book, and the publishers apologise for any inadvertent omissions.
Pie Corbett for the use of *Greedy Fox, The Little Red Hen, Monkey See! Monkey Do!* retold by Pie Corbett © 2008, Pie Corbett (2008, previously unpublished).
Chris Heald for the use of *The Golden Goose* retold by Chris Heald © 2008, Chris Heald (2008, previously unpublished)
Vivian French for the use of *The Fox and the Stork* retold by Vivian French from 'Aesop's Funky Fables' © 1997, (1997, Puffin) Vivian French (2008).
Helen East for the use of *Monkey and Turtle* retold by Helen East © 2008, Helen East (2008, previously unpublished).
Jane Grell for the use of *Ananse and the Golden Box of Stories* retold by Jane Grell © 2008, Jane Grell (2008, previously unpublished).
Xanthe Gresham for the use of *The Holy Man* retold by Xanthe Gresham © 2008, Xanthe Gresham (2008, previously unpublished).
Hugh Lupton for the use of *The Udala Tree* from *Early Years Activity Bank - September 2006* © 2006, Hugh Lupton (2006, Scholastic) and *The Three Sillies* from *Scholastic Collections: Tales, Myths and Legends* compiled by Pie Corbett, both retold by Hugh Lupton ©1993, Hugh Lupton (1993, Scholastic).
Mary Medlicott for the use of *The Door in the Mountain* retold by Mary Medlicott © 2008, Mary Medlicott (2008, previously unpublished).
Jess Smith for the use of *Tommy and the Elves* retold by Jess Smith © 2008, Jess Smith (2008, previously unpublished).
Taffy Thomas for the use of *The Cat's Drum, Farmer Merryweather's Cow, Why Dog Lives with Man* and *The Gingerbreadman* all retold by Taffy Thomas © 2008, Taffy Thomas (2008, previously unpublished).
The publishers would like to thank Xanthe Gresham, Pie Corbett and Taffy Thomas for their readings on the audio CD and also Linden Studios and Adrian Moss for the audio CD development.

THE GINGERBREAD MAN

And other stories for 4-7 year olds

Compiled by

PIE CORBETT

SCHOLASTIC

Introduction

Three golden apples fall from heaven –
one is for the person who tells the tale;
one is for the person who listens;
and one is for the person who passes it on.

Storytelling weaves a spell that binds us all into one world community. We enter that other world where anything is possible and we can think, feel and grow together. Stories help sustain and create our community. They help to fashion who we are and to know what is right and what is wrong. Stories cherish the human spirit within ourselves and within the children who listen to and tell them.

All cultures have songs, art, dance, religion – and of course, stories. Without the stories of our culture, we have no culture.

Research has shown that children who are read to and hear stories before going to school are the most likely to succeed in school. This is because stories help children to sit still, listen and concentrate; they also help to develop abstract thinking so that children who have had stories told or read to them are the first to form abstract concepts across the curriculum. In addition, stories create a comforting imaginative world in which ogres can be confronted and our deepest fears played out and controlled.

It is worth noticing how the most proficient writers in any class are readers. They are children who were probably read to before they went to school, have a bedtime story every night and have become avid readers themselves. This constant repetition of listening to and reading stories has helped them internalise the patterns they need to create stories of their own. Because you cannot create stories out of nothing.

Pie Corbett 2008

The Holy Man

Retold by Xanthe Gresham

Once upon a time there was a little black cat who had a cough.

"Oh no!" He thought that he should keep warm. So he got closer and closer to the fire, until – "*Meow!*" – he singed his fur.

"That does it. I'm going to go and see the holy man on the other side of the mountain to see if he can cure my cough." So off he went on his way.

Meow, meow, meow.

He hadn't gone very far – in fact only to the first bend in the road – when who should he meet but a little red hen.

"Where are you going?" said the hen.

"I'm going to see the holy man on the other side of the mountain because I've got a cough," said the cat.

"That's very funny, because I've got a cough too, you know. Can I come?"

"The more the merrier!" said the cat. So off they went on their way.

Meow, cluck, cluck, meow, cluck, cluck, meow, cluck, cluck.

When, they got to the next bend in the road, who should they meet but a golden cow.

"Where are you going?" said the cow.

"Well, we don't feel very well. I've got a cough and so's my friend the little red hen," said the cat, "and we're going to the holy man on the other side of the mountain, to see if he can cure our coughs."

"That's very funny," said the cow, "because I've got a cough too, you know. Can I come?"

"The more the merrier!" said the cat.

"*Cluck*," said the little red hen. "*Cluck*, I suppose so." So off they went on their way.

Meow, cluck, cluck, moo, meow, cluck, cluck, moo, meow, cluck, cluck, moo.

They got to the next bend in the road and who should be standing there but a white woolly sheep.

"Where are you going?" said the sheep.

"I don't feel very well," said the cat. "I've got a cough, and so have my friends the little red hen and the golden cow and we're going to the holy man on the other side of the mountain, to see if he can cure our coughs."

"That's very funny, because I've got a cough too, you know. Can I come?"

"The more the merrier!" said the cat. So off they went on their way.

Meow, cluck, cluck, moo, baaa, meow, cluck, cluck, moo, baaa, meow, cluck, cluck, moo, baa.

They walked and they walked, and they walked and they walked, they walked till they got to the top of the first hill and it started to get dark.

The crows were flying to the wood, the bats were whirling around their heads, and the little red hen said, "I don't like the dark."

"I don't like the dark," said the sheep.

"I don't like the dark either," said the cat.

"Oh, pull yourselves together," said the cow. "Look down in the valley. I can see a house with a spiral of smoke. That means there might be help. Sheep, get on

my back, cat get on the back of sheep,
little red hen get on the back of cat.

Now hold on very tight because
we're going to go very, very, very, very,
very, very fast."

*Meow, cluck, cluck, moo, baaa, meow,
cluck, cluck, moo, baaa, meow, cluck,
cluck, moo, baa.*

They landed in a heap at the bottom
of the hill, right up against the window

of the house. The cat looked in the window and what should he see, but a little old lady. She was rocking backwards and forwards on her chair.

"Oh, deary, deary me. Oh deary, deary me. I'm too much alone. If only I had a little black cat to sit on my lap, if only I had a little red hen to lay me an egg, and if only I had a golden cow, I could have a cup of tea.

"But, oh deary, deary me, no tea and that's the last bit of firewood. And I'm just too old and too cold to get any more."

On the back of the sheep that was on the back of the cow, the little black cat looked up at the little red hen and said, "You know, I haven't got a cough any more – extraordinary!"

"I don't seem to have a cough either," said the little red hen.

"How strange, I seem to have lost my

cough as well" said the sheep.

"Oh, for goodness sake, I never had a cough in the first place," said the cow, "and neither did you, hen, and neither did you, sheep." And the cow went forward and knocked on the door with his golden horns.

"Visitors!" said the little old lady. "For *me*? How exciting!"

She opened the door and in came the little black cat with his tail straight

up. She sat down and the little black cat sat on her lap. Gently, it ran its claws along her apron, "*Purrr, purrr.*" The little red hen went "*cluck, cluck,*" and laid an egg! And the golden cow said, "Well, does anyone want a cup of tea, because I need milking. Come on!"

So they had a cup of tea, and then the white woolly sheep said, "Why don't you take a bit of my wool and knit yourself a jumper, because you know that's the last bit of firewood."

And that's exactly what the old lady did, and they never got to see the holy man on the other side of the mountain. He was probably very good, but they were happy just where they were.

Why Dog Lives With Man

Retold by Taffy Thomas

Dog used to live on his own. But Dog got lonely. He thought he needed a friend.

Just then Dog spotted Hare. Dog thought that Hare could be his friend. Dog went over to Hare and said, "You and me could be friends."

Hare said, "OK, we'll give it a go." In the daytime, Dog and Hare went hunting together and at night they lay side by side. But in the middle of the night, Dog woke up and howled. . .

"*HOWWWWWWWWL!*"

Hare said, "Don't do that. If you do that you'll wake up Wolf, and Wolf will come and kill us."

Dog reasoned that if Hare was frightened of Wolf, then Wolf must be the tougher. If this was the case then perhaps Dog should have Wolf as his friend.

Dog went over to Wolf and said, "Hey, you and me could be friends."

Wolf said, "OK, we'll give it a go."

So in the daytime, Dog and Wolf went hunting together and at night they lay side by side. But in the middle of the night, Dog woke up and howled. . .

"HOWWWWWWWWWL!"

Wolf said, "Don't do that! If you do that you'll wake up Bear, and Bear will come and kill us."

Dog reasoned that if Wolf was frightened of Bear, then Bear must be the tougher. If this was the case then perhaps Dog should have Bear as his friend.

Dog went over to Bear and said, "Hey, you and me could be friends."

Bear said, "OK, we'll give it a go."

So in the daytime, Dog and Bear went hunting together and at night they lay side by side. But in the middle of the night, dog woke up and howled. . .

"*HOWWWWWWWWL!*"

Bear said, "Don't do that! If you do that you'll wake up Man, and Man will come and kill us."

Dog reasoned that if Bear was frightened of Man, then Man must be the tougher. If this was the case then perhaps Dog should have Man as his friend.

Dog went over to Man and said, "Hey, you and me could be friends."

Man said, "OK, we'll give it a go."

So in the daytime, Dog and Man went hunting together and at night they lay side by side. But in the middle of the night, dog woke up and howled...

"HOWWWWWWWWWL!"

Man said, "That's great! If you keep doing that you'll scare away Hare, Wolf, Bear, and burglars, and for that you can stay in my house and I'll feed you."

And ever since that day Dog and Man have been the best of friends.

The Gingerbread Man

Retold by Taffy Thomas

Opposite the storyteller's Garden is Sarah Nelson's famous gingerbread shop because Grasmere is the gingerbread capital of the world. However, when the local children take part in the summer Rushbearing Festival, the gingerbread they are given is more like ginger cake, and is made by the village baker. When Taffy settled in Grasmere in 1980, the baker was Colin Hilton. This is his story.

One day, Colin the baker was feeling lonely, so he mixed up a very special gingerbread dough. He took a handful of the mixture and rolled it into a sausage to make the body, and put it on the tray. He rolled another handful into a ball and popped it above the body to make the head. He took one last handful and rolled it into a long thin sausage to make the arms and the legs. He put these in

place and squashed it flat. Popping the
tray into the oven, he went upstairs and
had a cup of tea.

When he came down again, he could
hear a tap-tap-tapping coming from
inside the oven. He opened the oven
door and standing on the edge of the
tray was a little gingerbread man, who
jumped out and ran around the room
saying,

"Run, run, as fast as you can.
You can't catch me,
I'm the gingerbread man."

Colin the baker began to chase him, and again he said,

"Run, run, as fast as you can.
You can't catch me,
I'm the gingerbread man."

The little gingerbread man ran into the shop. Who should be in the shop but Taffy's two daughters, Aimee and Rosie. Aimee, a very good girl, always leaves doors open. The gingerbread man ran out of the door, turned left and started running towards the Tourist Information Centre, chased by Aimee, Rosie and Colin the baker. And the little gingerbread man said,

"Run, run, as fast as you can.
You can't catch me,
I'm the gingerbread man."

The woman who works in the
Tourist Information Centre is called Mrs
Rickman. She raced out of the shop; and
the grannies and grandpas came out of
the old folks' home – some in their
wheelchairs – and chased the
gingerbread man towards St Oswald's
church. Running towards the church was

Aimee, Rosie, Colin the baker, Mrs Rickman and the grannies and grandpas in their wheelchairs.

The verger, who looks after the church, is called Bob, and he has a big black dog called Sweep. When the dog saw the gingerbread man, he licked his chops and gave chase, pulling Bob along on the end of the lead. The gingerbread man headed towards the village school, chased by Aimee, Rosie, Colin the baker, Mrs Rickman, the grannies and grandpas in their wheelchairs, Bob, and Sweep the dog. And the gingerbread man said,

"Run, run, as fast as you can.
You can't catch me,
I'm the gingerbread man."

Mike, the headmaster, was looking out of the window. He rushed out and joined the chase as the gingerbread man headed towards the Wordsworth Museum – Dove Cottage – once the home of the famous poet William Wordsworth, long ago. Running towards the Museum was the gingerbread man, chased by Aimee, Rosie, Colin the baker, Mrs Rickman, the grannies and grandpas in their wheelchairs, Bob, Sweep the dog, and Mike the headmaster. The curator of the museum is called Terry, and he has two boys, Rowan and Tangwyn. They came out and joined the chase.

Across Lake Grasmere, and he could climb over Red Bank and escape into Langdale, the next valley. Running towards the lake was the gingerbread man, chased by Aimee, Rosie, Colin the baker, Mrs Rickman, the grannies and grandpas in their wheelchairs, Bob, Sweep the dog, Mike the headmaster, Rowan and Tangwyn. And the gingerbread man said,

"Run, run, as fast as you can.
You can't catch me,
I'm the gingerbread man."

Standing on the edge of the lake was a red-haired fox – a vixen. She licked her chops as the gingerbread man ran towards her.

"Can you swim?" asked the gingerbread man.

"Certainly," said the vixen. So the

gingerbread man jumped on her back and she paddled into the lake.

She swam towards the island in the middle, the water splashed on to the vixen's back, and the gingerbread man leapt onto her head. The gingerbread man was still getting splashed, and there's nothing worse than soggy gingerbread. He tugged her ears, pulling her nose towards the sky, and leapt onto the tip of it. He thought he was safe for he could see all the people who had chased him stuck on the shore, shaking their fists.

However, the vixen was crafty and as she reached the island, she tossed her nose and flicked the gingerbread man into the air. As he fell, she caught him in her jaws … and ate him.

Farmer Merryweather's Cow

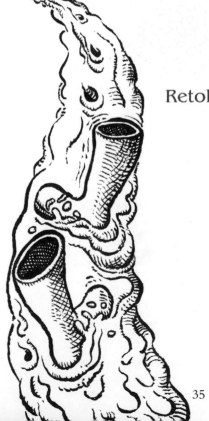

Retold by Taffy Thomas

Now did I tell you about the iron winter? In the iron winter the snow in the Lake District didn't melt until the 1st July! When it did melt the farmers had to borrow ladders to get their sheep down from the treetops. But I won't. I'll tell you about the soggy spring, when the frogs wore flippers, goats wore galoshes, water voles wore wetsuits and Farmer Merryweather's cow got stuck in the mud.

She was stuck in the mud from her buttocks to her bonce. Farmer Merryweather was worried. He took two hand-turns of her tail. . .

...and he tugged
and he twisted
and he pulled.
But he could not pull that cow out
of the mud.

Luckily Bessy Blood the butcher was passing, and she came to help. So Bessy Blood held on to Farmer Merryweather and Farmer Merryweather on to the cow. . .

. . .and he tugged
and he twisted
and he pulled.
But they could not pull that cow out
of the mud.

Luckily, Billy Bun the baker was passing, and he came to help. So Billy Bun the baker held on to Bessy Blood, Bessy Blood held on to Farmer

Merryweather and Farmer
Merryweather on to the cow. . .

*. . .and he tugged
and he twisted
and he pulled.
But they could not pull that cow
out of the mud.*

Luckily, Patricia the postie was
passing, and she came to help. So Patricia
the postie held on to Billy Bun, Billy
Bun held on to Bessy Blood, Bessy
Blood held on to Farmer Merryweather
and Farmer Merryweather held on to
the cow. . .

. . .and he tugged
and he twisted
and he pulled.
But they could not pull that cow out
of the mud.

Suddenly, there was a loud *snap*! And they all fell on their bottoms in the mud! Except the cow who was still stuck.

Now if that tail had been a little bit stronger. . .

. . .this tale would have been a little bit longer.

The Cat's Drum

Retold by Taffy Thomas

Not many people know this, but the first pussycat on this earth had a drum.

A naughty rat stole the cat's drum. The cat chased the rat and caught up with it in the corner of a barn. The rat started shaking as the cat got ready to pounce.

The rat realised it could only save itself by whirling the drum around its head and throwing it at the cat, hitting it on the nose. Whilst the cat was confused the rat could escape.

The rat whirled the drum around its head and threw it at the cat. However, the cat's mouth was open and the drum went right inside.

The pussycat swallowed the drum. Ever since that day, every cat on this earth has had a drum in their tummy. If you want to play the cat's drum, you

don't have to bash it with your hands like a set of bongos. You don't even have to bash it with sticks like the drummer from your favourite pop group or your school band!

All you have to do is to put the pussycat on your lap, roll it on its back and stroke its tummy. If you do this, it will go "*prrrrrrrrr*".

So that is how you play the cat's drum and why pussycats make the noise that we call purring.

Greedy Fox

Retold by Pie Corbett

Early one morning Mr Fox woke up. He picked up his bag and went out to visit his lady friend.

He walked and he walked and he walked till he came to the town pond. There he saw a frog.

"*Mmmm*," he thought, "that would make a nice present." So, he grabbed the frog and popped it into his bag.

He walked and he walked and he walked till he came to the candlestick maker's shop. He knocked on the door and went straight in.

He said to the candlestick maker, "May I leave my bag here while I visit my uncle?"

"Of course you can," said the candlestick maker.

"Very well," said Mr Fox, "but there is one thing. While I am gone, mind you don't look in my bag." Then he walked down the path, turned the corner and disappeared out of sight.

However, the candlestick maker grew curious. He opened the bag and out hopped the frog! A large brown rat pounced onto the frog and ate it up in one huge gulp.

Unfortunately, at that moment, back came Mr Fox. "Where is my frog?"

"I'm sorry," said the candlestick maker, "I opened up your bag and it hopped out, and that large brown rat ate it up!"

"Right," said Mr Fox. "I'll have the rat instead." So he grabbed the rat, shoved it into the bag and off he went.

He walked and he walked and he

walked till he came to the baker's shop. He knocked on the door and went straight in.

He said to the baker, "May I leave my bag here while I visit my uncle? But there is one thing. While I am gone, mind you don't look in my bag." Then he walked down the path, turned the corner and disappeared out of sight.

However, the baker grew curious. He opened the bag and out shot the rat! It shot out into the backyard and was chased off by the baker's puppy!

Unfortunately, at that moment, back came Mr Fox. "Where is my rat?"

"I'm sorry," said the baker. "I opened up your bag and it ran out into the backyard. My puppy chased it off!"

"Right," said Mr Fox. "I'll have your puppy instead." So he grabbed the puppy, shoved it into the bag and off he went.

He walked and he walked and he walked till he came to the butcher's shop. He knocked on the door and went straight in.

He said to the butcher, "May I leave my bag here while I visit my uncle? But there is one thing. While I am gone, mind you don't look in my bag." Then he walked down the path, turned the corner and disappeared out of sight.

However, the butcher grew curious. He opened the bag and out shot the puppy! It ran into the farmyard and was chased off by a little boy – *whack, whack*!

Unfortunately, at that moment, back came Mr Fox. "Where is my puppy?"

"I'm sorry," said the butcher. "I

opened the bag and it ran out into the farmyard and my boy chased it off!"

"Right," said Mr fox. "I'll have … some meat instead." So he grabbed a leg of lamb that was on the table, shoved it into the bag and off he went.

He walked and he walked and he

walked. Before long, the dogs of the town began to follow him, one by one. They could smell the fresh meat in the bag. Soon he had twenty dogs following him, then thirty dogs, then forty. They

began barking at his heels, so he ran and
he ran and he ran.

Out of the town, out of the town.
Over the down, over the down.
Across the lea, across the lea.
Down to the sea, down to the sea.

And as far as I know, Mr Fox is still
running to this day, still chased by that
pack of dogs.

The Little Red Hen

Retold by Pie Corbett

Once upon a time there was a little red hen who lived on a farm.

Early one morning she woke up and went outside. There she found some corn.

"Who will help me plant the corn?" said the little red hen.

"Not I," said the bull.

"Not I," said the cat.

"Not I," said the rat.

"Oh very well, I'll do it myself," said the little red hen – and so she did!

"Who will help me water the corn?" said the little red hen.

"Not I," said the bull.

"Not I," said the cat.

"Not I," said the rat.

"Oh very well, I'll do it myself," said the little red hen – and so she did!

"Who will help me cut the corn?"

said the little red hen.

"Not I," said the bull.

"Not I," said the cat.

"Not I," said the rat.

"Oh very well, I'll do it myself," said the little red hen – and so she did!

"Who will help me carry the corn to the mill?" said the little red hen.

"Not I," said the bull.

"Not I," said the cat.

"Not I," said the rat.

"Oh very well, I'll do it myself," said the little red hen — and so she did!

"Who will help me grind the corn?" said the little red hen.

"Not I," said the bull.

"Not I," said the cat.

"Not I," said the rat.

"Oh very well, I'll do it myself," said the little red hen — and so she did!

"Who will help me knead the bread?" said the little red hen.

"Not I," said the bull.

"Not I," said the cat.

"Not I," said the rat.

"Oh very well, I'll do it myself," said the little red hen — and so she did!

"Who will help me bake the bread?" said the little red hen.

"Not I," said the bull.

"Not I," said the cat.

"Not I," said the rat.

"Oh very well, I'll do it myself," said the little red hen — and so she did!

"Who will help me eat the bread?" said the little red hen.

"I will," said the bull.

"I will," said the cat.

"I will," said the rat.

"Oh no you won't. I'll eat it myself," said the little red hen — and so she did!

The Three Sillies

Retold by Hugh Lupton

Once upon a time there lived a man and his name was John. One day he was walking along the road, and the sun was shining, and he was thirsty. And there, beside the road, was a pub. So he pushed open the door, went inside and called to the landlord, "Landlord, landlord, a pint of beer, please!"

And the landlord called to his daughter Betsy, "Betsy, go down the cellar and fetch a pint of beer for this gentleman, will you."

And so down the cellar stairs went Betsy.

Well, John waited and waited and waited, but no pint of beer came.

"Landlord," he said, "what happened to my pint of beer?"

"Didn't Betsy bring it to you?"

"No, she did not."

"Well then, she must be down the cellar still."

So down the cellar stairs they went. And there was Betsy, with tears streaming down her face, howling and wailing, "Oh dear, oh dear, oh dear, oh dear…"

"What's the matter?" says John.

Betsy shakes her head, choking on her sobs and spluttering to find the words, "Oh dear, oh dear. You see, I came down the cellar to fetch a pint of beer, and I looked up and I saw that axe…" She pointed up to where an axe is stuck in a beam in the ceiling.

"…And I fell to thinking… oh dear, oh dear, what if one day I got married… oh dear, oh dear, and what if I had five children… oh dear, dear me, and what if the smallest one of them children had a cat… oh deary me, and what if that cat had five kittens… oh dear, oh dear, and what if one dreadful day, the smallest one of them five kittens came down the cellar stairs… oh dear, oh dear, and what if, just at that moment, that axe … oh dear … what if it fell out of the beam … and … chopped off the end of its tail… oh dear, oh dear, oh dear."

Well, John couldn't believe his ears. "I've heard some unlikely stories in my time, but that must be the unlikeliest," he said. "And I've met some silly people but you must be the silliest. In fact," he said, turning to the landlord, "in fact, if I was ever to meet three people more silly than your daughter Betsy, I'll tell you what, I'd come right back here and I'd marry her!"

Well, the landlord grinned and he nodded and he shook John by the hand, and Betsy dabbed her eyes with a hanky and smiled through her tears, and she poured John a pint of the best beer. And John drank the beer, climbed the cellar stairs, and set off on his travels.

Well, he travelled here and he travelled there, and he travelled there and he travelled here. Then one day as he was walking through a village, he saw a wonderful sight.

You see, all the roofs of the houses were thatched, and there was one house where the thatch was so old and rotten that grass had begun to grow on it. Now, an old woman had pushed a ladder up against that house, and she was trying to persuade her cow to climb the ladder and eat the grass.

"Go on, Daisy, climb up the ladder,"

she was shouting and scolding. "Go on, Daisy, and climb up the ladder."

But have you ever seen a cow climb up a ladder? She was thumping the cow, and the cow was stamping and champing.

"Go on, Daisy, climb up the ladder!"

"*Mooooooo.*"

And John stood and he stared and he couldn't believe his eyes; and as he watched he was thinking to himself, "There's somebody even sillier than the landlord's daughter Betsy, so that makes *one.*"

Well, he travelled here and he travelled there, and he travelled there and he travelled here. And one night he had to stay in a hotel and as he was lying in his bed, he saw a wonderful sight. You see, the hotel was crowded, and so he was sharing a room with another man. And early in the morning, he was woken by the strangest sound.

Boing … boing … boing … "Bother!"
Boing … boing … boing … "Bother!"

And John opened his eyes and looked across the room, and there was the other man jumping on his bed; and tied up between the bedposts were his trousers. He was trying to jump into his trousers!

But have you ever tried jumping into a pair of trousers? He kept missing, and he had to climb up on to the bed and try again.

Boing … boing … boing … "Bother!"

And John lay and he watched and he couldn't believe his eyes. And then he climbed out of the bed.

"Excuse me," he said, "but there's a much easier way of putting on your trousers than that. You just hold them in your hands like this, put one foot down there, the other foot down there, heave them up, do the button, pull the zip and there you are."

"What a good idea!" said the other man. "I've never thought of that. For forty years I've been putting my trousers on like this. It takes me hours every morning. Now … it'll take me no time at all!"

And John stood and listened and thought to himself, "There's somebody even sillier than the landlord's daughter Betsy, so that makes *two*"

Well, he travelled here and he

travelled there, and he travelled there and he travelled here. And then, one evening he was walking and he saw a wonderful sight.

You see, there was a full moon shining in the sky, and beside the road there was a pond. And leaning over the pond was an old man with a long white beard. He was holding a fishing net in his hand, and he kept dipping it in the water and then peering into it.

"I didn't catch her that time... I didn't catch her that time, neither... Nor didn't I catch her that time, neither..."

John stood and he stared and he couldn't believe his eyes.

"Excuse me," he said, "but what are you doing?"

And the old man looked across at John and shook his head. "Stranger, a terrible thing has happened. The moon's gone and fallen into this here pond, and

I'm trying to fish her out so I can throw her back up into the sky!"

Have you ever tried fishing for the moon? The old man was dipping and peering and shaking his head. And John went across and caught the old man by the arm.

"Look into the sky," he said, "and tell me what you see." And the old man craned his neck and looked up into the sky. "That's funny, the moon's up there and the moon's down here."

And John left him standing by the pond in the moonlight, scratching his head. And as he walked away, he was thinking to himself, "There's somebody else even sillier than the landlord's daughter Betsy, and that makes *three*."

And so it came about that John married Betsy. It was a lovely wedding... and I wish you'd been there!

And do you know, John and Betsy

had five children.

And do you know, the smallest of those children had a cat.

And do you know, that cat had five kittens.

And do you know, one day the smallest of those five kittens went down the cellar stairs.

And do you think that axe fell out of the beam and chopped off the end of its tail?

Well … it didn't!

The Fox and the Stork

Aesop retold
by Vivian French

Fox was making soup – a mouth-watering, nose-twitching, stomach-filling soup.

"*Hmm*! A pinch of salt," he said to himself, "just one more pinch of salt and it'll be done. Oh! How I shall enjoy my soup! How I shall slurp my soup! How I shall smack my lips and rub my stomach!"

Fox stopped stirring. "What a shame there is no one to admire my magnificent cooking! Maybe I should invite someone to share my soup and dine with me."

Fox sat down to think. "I won't ask Lion," he decided, "because Lion would gobble all the soup at a gulp, and there would be none left for me. And I won't invite Dog or Cat because they would eat at least half. And I won't invite Bluebottle because of her buzz. Besides, she would put her feet in the food."

Fox went on thinking. "*Hmm... Hmm... Hmm...* I know!" He leapt up. "I'll invite my dear friend Stork! Stork is a bird of fine feathers and feelings – Stork will be the ideal guest!" And Fox went hurrying out to invite his friend.

Stork was pleased to come. She bowed in the doorway, and thanked Fox for his kindness.

"What a delicious smell! Mr Fox, what a wonderful cook you must be. I am most honoured to be asked to share your soup!"

Fox bowed back, and grinned a foxy grin. As he bowed he was thinking snidey, slidey, foxy thoughts...

"Aha!" he said to himself. "Mrs Stork loves the smell of my soup! But if she loves the taste she might eat too long and too well! Let me see... Let me see... Aha!"

Fox hurried to set the table. He set a wide flat dish for himself, and a wide flat dish for Mrs Stork. Mrs Stork watched him, and her shiny little black eyes winked and blinked as she saw what Fox was doing.

"Do be seated, dear friend," Fox said, and he began to ladle the soup on to the plates. "Such hot soup! But you will find it cools quickly. See! I can eat mine

now!" And Fox lapped up his soup with a flourish. "Ahaa! So delicious!"

Mrs Stork could eat nothing. Her long bill clicked and clacked against the dish, but not a drop of soup could she drink.

"Dear Mrs Stork!" Fox said. "Aren't you hungry? Dear me, dear me. Allow me to finish your soup for you... Waste not, want not, after all!"

Fox drank up Mrs Stork's soup with a loud slurp. Then he licked out the pan and polished the plates with his long red tongue.

"There!" said Mr Fox. He sat back,

his stomach bulging, and smacked his lips.

"Dear Mrs Stork," he said, "there is nothing as fine as sharing a meal with a friend." And he smiled his foxy smile.

Mrs Stork nodded. "You are quite right, Mr Fox," she said. "Indeed, you are right … so I hope you will join me for a meal tonight. It would give me such pleasure to return your kindness!"

Fox shuffled a little and pulled at his whiskers. His slippery thoughts slid round in his head. Was Mrs Stork staring a little coldly with her bright shining eyes? But a free meal was a free meal … and there was no soup left. Not a drip or a drop.

"I shall be delighted," Fox said. Mrs Stork bowed once more in the doorway. "Until tonight," she said. "And the pleasure will be all mine."

By the evening Fox was hungry

again. He leapt out of his house and trotted through the deep, dark woods to Mrs Stork's house. A wonderful smell was wafting out through the open window. Fox sniffed happily, and rubbed his stomach.

"Two fine dinners in a day!" he said and knocked at the door.

Mrs Stork smiled as she let Fox in.

"Do sit down, dear friend," she said.

Fox hurried to the table. He stopped and stared. The table was heaped high with mouth-watering, nose-twitching, stomach-filling food ... but every dish was tall and narrow.

"Just help yourself, dear friend!" said Mrs Stork. "Feel free to eat whatever you wish!" And she plunged her long thin beak into the tallest bowl.

Fox said nothing. His stomach was howling and growling with hunger, but Fox said nothing at all.

"Dear Mr Fox!" said Mrs Stork.
"Aren't you hungry? What a shame.
What a shame. Allow me to finish the
meal for you."

And she did.

Monkey and Turtle

Retold by
Helen East

One cold wet night, Monkey spotted Turtle, huddled under his tree.

"*Brrr*! Brother!" chattered Monkey. "You cold too?"

"*A-a-achoo*! F-f-frozen through. Whatever are we going to do?"

"*Mmm*", said Monkey. "I've been watching man. I don't know how he does it, but whatever the weather, he doesn't seem to mind."

"Ahhh," said Turtle. "Well, I suppose that's because he's got clothes. That's what we need too. I'll tell you what you should do. When morning comes and you can see, climb up into that coconut tree, tear off long, strong strips of bark and throw them down to me."

"That sounds like hard work," said Monkey."

"Yes," agreed Turtle, "but it'll keep

you warm."

"Fair enough," said Monkey. "But then you must put the bark in the clean stream water, and trample it down, walking round and round to make it flat, and soften into cloth."

"That sounds like hard work," said Turtle.

"Yes," agreed Monkey, "but it'll keep you warm."

"That's true," said Turtle. "But then Monkey, with your clever fingers you'll have to sew the cloth into clothes."

"Only when you, Turtle, with your heavy jaws, have snapped each piece into shape."

"It will be hard work!" they both sighed – but then they brightened up. "It will warm us up all right!"

So all night long, they planned, and talked about the clothes they would have. But when morning came and the sun

rose, the rain stopped, and the forest
warmed up. The monkey and the turtle
began to relax in the heat, they settled
themselves, and went to sleep.

By and by the turtle stirred. "Hey,
Monkey!" he called. "Weren't you going
to get busy tearing bark cloth off your
tree?"

The monkey opened one lazy eye.
"Me? Work that hard? But why?"

"Well… It would keep you warm…" Turtle began.

"Silly idea. I'm just fine as I am. But Turtle, hey, weren't you going to rush round and round, softening the cloth, and trampling it down?"

"Whatever for?"

"Well … to keep you warm."

"That's the last thing I need in this heat."

As for the clothes – who needed those? Certainly not when it was this hot! "Ridiculous!" they both agreed.

And off they went to take their ease, and dabble and paddle in the cooling stream…

Until the wind turned, the sun sank, and the rain returned, the cold came back. Then Monkey called again to his turtle friend, "Hey, you cold too? What are we going to do?"

And you know what they agreed,

don't you?

So it happened every night, so it happened every day, so it happens still, they say, because some things will never change!

The Udala Tree

Retold by Hugh Lupton

Astory, a story! Let it go, let it come!

There was a little girl and her name was Sia Jetta. She lived with her two big brothers in a hut, in a village in West Africa.

Every day she had to work. She had to work very hard.

She had to sweep the yard.

She had to milk the goats.

She had to hoe the field.

She had to feed the chickens.

She had to pound the yams.

She had to run to the well for water.

She had to cook the food.

And as for her two brothers – they did nothing. They sat in the sunshine and watched her working.

And when she put food onto the table at the end of the day those two brothers would grab the best of it, so that, as often as not, she went to bed hungry.

That was the way it was.

Then one time, as she was hoeing in the field, Sia Jetta found a seed. She found a little, shiny seed lying on the ground. She picked it up between her finger and thumb.

"You belong to me," she said. "You belong to nobody but me." She put it into her pocket.

When she went to bed at the end of the day, she put the seed under her pillow. That night she had a dream. She dreamed that an udala tree grew out of the seed and spread its branches and leaves high over her head.

So, early the next morning she went out into the garden and planted it. She fetched water from the well and watered it.

Then Sia Jetta began to sing:

"*Udala tree grow!*
(clap)
Grow for Sia Jetta!
(clap)
Udala tree grow!
(clap)
Grow for Sia Jetta!
(clap)
This earth is a place of call.
(clap)
We stop here and go on.
(clap)"

Straight away a little green shoot pushed up out of the soil. It grew and grew, it hardened and darkened, and soon a great tree trunk stretched high above her head.

"Udala tree branch!
(clap)
A branch for Sia Jetta!
(clap)
Udala tree branch!
(clap)
Branch for Sia Jetta!
(clap)
This earth is a place of call.
(clap)
We stop here and go on.
(clap)"

Boughs and branches pushed out of the trunk and spread themselves across the sky above her head.

"Udala tree leaf!
(clap)
Leaf for Sia Jetta!
(clap)
Udala tree leaf!
(clap)
Leaf for Sia Jetta!
(clap)
This earth is a place of call.
(clap)
We stop here and go on.
(clap)"

Suddenly, fresh green leaves rustled and whispered and threw a cool shade over her head and shoulders.

"Udala tree fruit!
(clap)
Fruit for Sia Jetta!
(clap)

Udala tree fruit!
(clap)
Fruit for Sia Jetta!
(clap)
This earth is a place of call.
(clap)
We stop here and go on.
(clap)"

And the branches above her head were covered with yellowy-pink udala fruit.

"Udala tree drop!
(clap)
Drop for Sia Jetta!
(clap)
Udala tree drop!
(clap)
Drop for Sia Jetta!
(clap)
This earth is a place of call.
(clap)
We stop here and go on.
(clap)"

And *plop, plop, plop* … all around her the fruit fell down to the ground. She picked them up and tore them open and gobbled down the delicious pink flesh and the sweet milky juice.

"Mmm."

It was just as she was eating that her brothers woke up. They climbed out of bed. They came out of the hut, rubbing

their eyes.

They saw a tree where there had never been a tree before! They saw Sia Jetta feasting on the fruit. She waved to them, "Come and help yourselves!" she said. They ran across to the tree and they began to eat.

"Eat as many as you like," she said, "but only the fruit that's fallen to the ground. You mustn't climb the tree. You must never climb the tree."

Well, all morning those two brothers ate. They ate while Sia Jetta worked. By the end of the morning, they'd eaten all of the udala fruit.

And did they want more? Of course they did.

Sia Jetta had gone to the well for water. Nobody was watching. They climbed up the trunk of the tree as nimbly as a couple of monkeys. They broke the branches and crammed the fruit into their mouths.

When Sia Jetta came back with the buckets of water, they were still up there.

Was she angry? She was furious!

She stood at the foot of the tree and began to sing:

"Udala tree grow!
(clap)
Grow for Sia Jetta!
(clap)
Udala tree grow!
(clap)
Grow for Sia Jetta!
(clap)
This earth is a place of call.
(clap)
We stop here and go on.
(clap)"

And the tree grew. It grew up and up. It grew higher and higher until those two brothers were in the sky, until they were lost in the clouds.

"Help!" they shouted.

"Stop!" they shouted.
"Let us down!"
But Sia Jetta was angry.

"Udala tree grow!
(clap)
Grow for Sia Jetta!
(clap)
Udala tree grow!
(clap)

Grow for Sia Jetta!
(clap)
This earth is a place of call.
(clap)
We stop here and go on.
(clap)"

Now the top branches of the tree were touching the moon. All the people of the village came out to see what was happening. They craned their necks to catch a glimpse of the two brothers. They cupped their hands behind their ears to hear what they were saying.

"Let us down and we'll sweep the yard."

"Let us down and we'll milk the goats."

"Let us down and we'll hoe the field."

"Let us down and we'll feed the chickens."

"Let us down and we'll pound the yams."

"Let us down and we'll fetch the water."

"Let us down and we'll cook the food."

"Promise?" shouted Sia Jetta.

"We promise!"

And all the people of the village nodded their heads. "A promise is a promise – and there's no breaking it."

So Sia Jetta sang:

"Udala tree shrink!
(clap)
Shrink for Sia Jetta!
(clap)
Udala tree shrink!
(clap)
Shrink for Sia Jetta!
(clap)
This earth is a place of call.

(clap)
We stop here and go on.
(clap)"

And the tree shrank down to its proper size.

The two brothers scrambled down to the ground … and they kept their promises, that day and every day afterwards.

That was the way it was.

And Sia Jetta shared her fruit with all the people of the village. She gave one to me once…*Mmm*, I wish you could have tasted it!

Ananse and the Golden Box of Stories

Retold by Jane Grell

Long, long ago, all the stories of the world belonged to Nyame, the god of all things. He kept them in a golden box, next to his royal stool and shared them with no one.

Little Ananse, the spiderman, woke up one morning, feeling very sorry for himself. He walked with a bit of a limp, and talked with a bit of a lisp. Everyone treated him like an insignificant, ugly little spider.

Ananse thought to himself, "Everyone loves a story. Now, if only I could get my hands on Nyame's box of stories, maybe I could get some respect around here."

It was no sooner thought than done. Ananse spun a web up to the sky and bowed low before Nyame, the god of all things.

"Oh great Nyame," he said, "please,

can I buy your stories?"

"Buy my stories?" said Nyame, puzzled. "Little Ananse wants to buy my stories?" The idea amused Nyame whose portly belly wobbled as he laughed. But Ananse persisted.

"Please, oh great and wise Nyame."

In the end, Nyame stopped laughing, drew himself up to his godly height and looked hard at Ananse.

"So you'd like to buy my stories, eh, Ananse, but can you pay my price?"

"What is your price?" asked Ananse.

"Well," said Nyame, "if you want my stories, you must bring me three things. First of all, bring me Osebo, the leopard of the terrible teeth. Secondly, bring me Mboro, the hornets who sting like fire. And thirdly, bring me Moatia, the fairy who is never seen. Bring me those three things Ananse and my stories shall be yours."

Ananse thanked Nyame, spun a web back to earth and set to work.

First of all, he went into the forest in search of Osebo. Flung over his shoulder was a nice, strong rope made of vine creepers.

The leopard, who saw him coming from a distance shouted, "Hey, Ananse, how did you know it's my dinner time?" Ananse replied, "Oh great Osebo, before you eat me, can we play this little game?" Because Ananse knew how fond Osebo was of playing games.

"Game, what game?" asked Osebo eagerly.

"It's called the binding game," explained Ananse. "With this rope I tie you by the legs like this and like that. Then I untie you and it's your turn to tie me up."

"Hurry up, then," said Osebo. "I'm hungry."

So Ananse tied Osebo tightly by his front and hind legs. But instead of releasing him, Ananse hung Osebo on the branch of a tree saying, "You are now ready to meet Nyame, the god of all things."

His next task was to find and catch Mboro, the hornets who sting like fire. Ananse took a calabash, or a gourd, which he filled with water. He cut a huge banana frond which he held over his head like an umbrella. When he found the hornets' nest, he sprinkled the water from the calabash over the hornets while chanting, "It's raining, raining, raining."

The hornets became flustered because they hated their wings getting wet and tattered. As they flew around in confusion, Ananse held out the empty calabash and said, "Come, come into my calabash where you will be nice and dry."

One by one they flew into Ananse's calabash — *Voop! Voop! Voop!* — to the very last hornet. Then Ananse closed the mouth of the calabash.

"You Mboro are ready to meet Nyame, the god of all things," and he hung the gourd full of hornets next to Osebo, the leopard.

The third and final task, the most difficult of all, was to find and catch Moatia, the fairy who is never seen. Ananse sat under a huge flamboyant tree, in full bloom, and prayed for inspiration. It was believed that under this tree, the fairy Moatia came to dance.

Ananse carved a little wooden doll holding a bowl. He filled the bowl with soft white yams floating in rich, red butter. He then covered the doll with sticky latex gum and placed her at the foot of the tree. Ananse tied a string round the doll's neck. He took the other end of the string behind the tree where he crouched, hiding. Then he waited and waited and waited.

Ananse waited for what seemed like a hundred years. Eventually he heard the fairy Moatia come dancing, dancing, dancing, underneath the flamboyant tree. She stopped in her tracks when she saw

the sticky wooden doll holding the bowl of yams.

"Hello, gum baby," she said. "Can I have some of your yams? I'm so hungry." From his hiding place, Ananse tugged at the string and the doll seemed to nod, "Yes."

So Moatia the fairy ate every morsel of the yams and licked the bowl clean. Then she said, "Thank you, gum baby, that was delicious," but the doll made no move in reply. Moatia got cross.

"I think you're very rude, gum baby. If someone thanks you, you don't just sit there, ignoring them. I think I ought to teach you a lesson."

So saying, the fairy slapped the doll's face with her right hand, which got stuck fast.

"Let go of me or I'll give you another one." She slapped it with her left hand and of course got even more stuck.

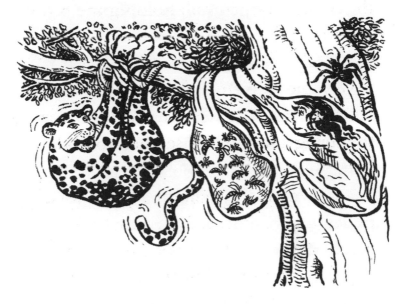

She kicked and wriggled, but only made matters worse. There was no escape for Moatia the fairy.

Ananse skipped from his hiding place. "You too, Moatia, are ready to meet Nyame, the god of all things," he said. He spun a fine net in which he scooped up the fairy, the hornets and the leopard. He hauled them up to the sky and lay them proudly before Nyame.

Well, even the great god Nyame was impressed. He called to his lords, ladies, underlings.

"Come round, gather round, come and see. Little Ananse, the spider, has bought me the price of my stories. From this day on, they shall be known as Ananse Stories." He then handed the golden box of stories to Ananse, who clutched it proudly and spun a web back to earth.

On his arrival in his village however – and no one knows quite why or how it happened – the golden box flew open and all the stories were scattered to almost every corner of the globe. Some of the stories went to the Caribbean, some went to America and some of them came to England. Many are still floating around today, looking for somewhere to go or someone to tell them. I think some of them might be in this room. Maybe Nyame is having the last laugh after all.

The Door in the Mountain

Retold by Mary Medlicott

One day, a girl called Betsi went up in the hills to play hide-and-seek with her friends. When it came to Betsi's turn for hiding, she decided to go further than they would ever find her.

She ran uphill and downhill until suddenly she stopped. For what do you think she saw, right there in front of her eyes? There was a door in the hill, and the door was open.

As soon as Betsi saw that door in the hill, she knew what she wanted to do. She went in. Behind the door was a dark, dark tunnel and when Betsi came out the other side of that tunnel, she found herself in a different world.

At the bottom of the hill, she saw a shining blue lake. In the middle of the lake was a small grassy island. And as soon as Betsi caught sight of that island, she knew what she wanted to do.

Luckily for Betsi, at the edge of the lake was exactly the thing that she needed – a boat. The little boat was painted blue outside and inside. In the bottom was a pair of red-painted oars.

Betsi climbed in the boat and pushed off from the shore. When she got to the island, she quickly climbed out. And what do you think she saw on that island as soon as she started looking about? Betsi saw the Tylwyth Teg.

They were very small, little people, and very pretty to look at. When they saw Betsi, they greeted her warmly, as if they'd been waiting for her.

"Welcome to our island, Betsi. Please do come to our party," they said.

There were plenty of good things to eat at the party and then there was music and dancing. A fiddler played Betsi her favourite song,

"Ffol-di-rol ho ho,
Ffol-di-rol ho ho,
Ffol-di-riddle, ffol-di-rol, ho ho."

After all the turning and swirling and whirling about, Betsi asked the little people if she could explore their island. Of course she could, the little people said. There was just one rule that she should keep.

"Don't pick any flowers on our

island," they said.

Well, on the island there was a wild fairy wood. When Betsi went into that wild fairy wood, she saw a thousand daffodils. They looked like a golden sea of flowers and they seemed to be calling her into their midst.

She waded in through the shimmering yellow. As she stood there, surrounded by flowers, she desperately

wanted to pick one. She looked to see which was the brightest and best. And when she saw it, she picked it. She picked the biggest, most beautiful daffodil.

And can you guess what happened then? As soon as Betsi picked that daffodil, she remembered what the little people had said,

"*Don't pick any flowers on our island, Betsi.*"

At that very moment, she remembered her friends. They would still be playing hide-and-seek. They would still be searching for her!

So Betsi started to run. Still holding the daffodil, she ran out of the wild fairy wood, she ran past the little people, she ran towards the little boat which she'd left at the edge of the lake. She was nearly there when she heard the little people shouting,

"You picked a flower on our island, Betsi!"

Still clutching the daffodil, Betsi ran faster. She jumped into the boat at the edge of the lake, rowed over the lake as fast as she could, climbed out of the boat and went back through the tunnel. Then she ran down the hillside to look for her friends. There was no one there. They must have all gone home.

When Betsi got back to her own house, her mother was making the

supper. She sounded a bit cross with Betsi.

"Betsi where *have* you been?" she said. "And where did you get that daffodil?"

"I'm not telling," Betsi replied.

And she didn't. Not for ages. By then, two very strange, magic things had happened.

The first was that the daffodil didn't wither or die like flowers usually do after they've been cut. Betsi put it in a bottle which she filled with water. She put the bottle on the kitchen table and whenever she looked at it, it was still bright golden yellow. It stayed that way for a long, long time.

The other strange thing was the door in the mountain. For whenever Betsi went back in the hills to try and find that door again, it wasn't there. However often she went and however hard she looked, she never managed to find it again.

But she didn't forget it either. Even when she got to be an old, old woman, she used to tell the story of it to whoever wanted to listen. And that's how I got to know the story and why I'm telling it to you today.

Tommy and the Elves

Retold by Jess Smith

I t was a sunny day. Little Tommy walked along the river and thought it would be nice to take a drink.

But what a shock he got when a teeny-weeny man wearing a green hat and pointed-toed boots popped his head out from a tree root by the river.

"What do you want?" said the teeny-weeny man.

"A drink of fresh water," replied Tommy in surprise.

"Not from my river."

"This is everyone's water."

"Well I'm a magical elf and I say who drinks water."

Tommy cupped his hands together to scoop up some water, but a strange thing happened – the water flowed out. He tried again, and the same thing happened. He told the elf to stop playing magic tricks.

"If you want a drink, pay me," demanded the elf.

Tommy had no money, so he asked, "What will you take instead?"

"Answer three questions."

"OK, what are they?"

"The first one is: how many trees are there in the forest? The second question is: how many stars are there in the night sky? And the last question is: what am I thinking?"

Tommy walked away. He was
unhappy and soon came upon another
elf who asked him why was he sad.
Tommy told him that Nasty Elf had
refused him a drink, and that he'd never
get one if he couldn't answer three
questions.

"What are they?" asked the nice elf, a
smiley-faced little man. Tommy told him.

The nice elf said that Squirrel was a

tree counter. He called Squirrel and asked him how many trees are there in the forest.

"I counted one thousand seven hundred and thirty-seven trees today." Tommy thanked Squirrel.

Question two was harder to answer, but Elf said, "Lily Frog lies on his back catching flies and counts stars." So he asked Lily Frog.

"Last night was a starry one. I counted too many," replied Lily Frog.

"That's no answer," said Tommy.

"There are too many to count."

For question three, Elf said, "Owl knows what everyone thinks. Let's ask him."

"That's easy," said Owl. "Nasty Elf thinks he's the cleverest elf in the world."

Tommy went to the river and met Nasty Elf again. "Have you got the answers?" he snapped.

"One thousand seven hundred and thirty-seven trees, billions of stars — count them if you don't believe me — and you are the cleverest of elves."

Nasty Elf was so angry; he jumped up and fell in the river. And Tommy was at last able to drink as much water as he wanted.

Monkey See, Monkey Do!

Retold by Pie Corbett

Once upon a time there was a hat seller. My, he had a hat for every occasion – fancy hats for weddings and broad-brimmed hats to keep the sun from your head.

One day he was travelling through the forest when his cart hit a stone in the road. Unfortunately, all the hats tipped onto the road.

As soon as the monkeys in the trees saw the hats, they swung down and picked them up as quick as a click.

First the hat seller yelled at the monkeys, but all that the monkeys did was to jabber back because –

what a monkey sees,
then a monkey does!

That made the hat seller really cross! Next the hat seller shook his fist at

the monkeys, but all that the monkeys
did was to shake their fists back,
because –

what a monkey sees,
then a monkey does!

That made the hat seller even more
cross!

After that the hat seller picked up a branch and threw it at the monkeys, but all that the monkeys did was to throw sticks back, because –

what a monkey sees,
then a monkey does!

The hat seller realised that he would never get his hats back!

Sadly, he rubbed his eyes and began to cry, but all that the monkeys did was to rub their eyes and cry, because –

what a monkey sees,
then a monkey does!

Eventually, the hat seller was so fed up that he threw his own hat onto the ground and stamped on it! Then he began to push his cart back towards the city. As he disappeared up the track, all that the monkeys did was to throw their hats onto the ground because –

what a monkey sees,
then a monkey does!

Luckily, the hat seller looked behind him and to his amazement all his hats were scattered back on the ground.

He looked up into the trees but there was not a monkey to be seen. They had all rushed off to another part of the forest where one of them had seen a gingerbread man being chased because –

what a monkey sees,
then a monkey does!

Four-leaf clover,
My story is over!

The Golden Goose

Retold by Chris Heald

Once upon a time there was a King who had just one daughter who he loved very much. However much her father tried to make her happy, the Princess could not smile and had never laughed like an ordinary girl. The King was very worried about her, so he proclaimed throughout the land that the first man to make his daughter smile would marry her and inherit half his kingdom.

On the other side of the kingdom lived a poor boy called Jack. He was a very kind boy who always tried to help people around him who were in need.

One day Jack was chopping wood when an old woman came along. She was crying and seemed very sad and upset.

"Don't cry," said Jack. "What's the matter? Can I do anything to help?"

"I am so hungry!" said the old woman. "I haven't had any food for three days, and I can't afford to buy any today either."

Now Jack had some food with him. It was not much, and it was all he had to eat for that day, but he was such a kind boy that that he gave all his food to the old woman because he felt so sorry for her.

When she had eaten, the old woman thanked Jack and told him to look for his reward in the hollow of a nearby tree. Then the old woman vanished.

Jack looked in the hollow tree and could not believe his eyes for there was the most wonderful goose he had ever

seen, a goose with feathers of pure gold.

"I must take this goose to show the King!" thought Jack, but the minute he took hold of the goose and lifted it up in his arms, his hands stuck fast to it and he could not let go, no matter how hard he tried.

"Oh well!" thought Jack, "I'll take this marvellous goose and go to see the King anyway." And away he went on the road to the King's palace.

The first place he came to was a

farm where the farmer's daughter was
bringing in the cows to milk. When she
saw Jack, she stopped what she was doing
and came to look at what he was
carrying.

"What a beautiful goose!" said the
farmer's daughter. "Do you think I could
have just one feather to keep?"

As I have said, Jack was a kind boy so
he said she could have a feather from the
golden goose, but as soon as the farmer's
daughter touched the goose, her hand
stuck fast to the feather and she could
not let go. She called to her mother for
help. "Mother, Mother, help me for I am
stuck to this goose."

"Don't be silly," said her mother.
"Who could be stuck to a goose? I'll
soon get you free!" and she grabbed her
daughter by the waist. As soon as she
touched her, she too stuck fast and could
not let go.

"Help! Help!" shouted the mother to her husband the farmer. "Help me for I am stuck to our daughter and cannot let go!"

When her husband heard her shouting, he left the pigs he was feeding and came running towards her. "Husband! Husband! Help me for I am stuck to this goose"

"Don't talk rubbish!" said the farmer. "Who could be stuck to a goose? I'll soon get you free!" and he got hold of his wife and pulled her away, but he too stuck fast and could not let go.

So there they were, Jack, the farmer's daughter, the farmer's wife and the farmer, all stuck fast to the golden goose.

"Well, I'm still going to see the King!" said Jack. "And it looks like you are all coming with me!"

The next place they came to was a mill by a stream. "What an amazing

goose!" said the miller's daughter. "Would you let me have just one feather to keep?"

"I wouldn't touch it if I were you!" said Jack, and the others all shouted, "*No!*" but it was too late. The miller's daughter had already touched the farmer, her hand was stuck fast to him and she could not let go.

She called to her brother for help. "Brother, Brother, help me for I am stuck to this goose."

"Don't be silly," said her brother. "Who could be stuck to a goose? I'll soon get you free!" and he grabbed his sister by the waist. As soon as he touched her, he too stuck fast and could not let go.

Soon they were walking along the road that led to the King's palace, and all the way along the road people were reaching out to touch the golden goose. Soon Jack had twenty people stuck to each other in a long line behind him and the goose.

Back at the palace the King was still worried about his daughter and the Princess had still not smiled on the day when Jack and his golden goose and all the people who were stuck entered the great hall of the palace.

The King was sitting on his throne with the Princess sitting beside him.

When the Princess saw all these people stuck together in a long line, tripping over each other and grumbling about their lot, a very strange thing happened. Her mouth began to curl upwards at the ends, she started to make strange noises in her throat.

The King leaned towards her, scared that she might be ill, when suddenly the Princess opened her mouth and the most amazing thing happened ... she *laughed*!

She didn't smile, she didn't grin, she laughed until tears ran down her face; she laughed until she slid off her throne and lay on the floor holding her aching sides. Her laughter broke the spell that had stuck everyone to the golden goose, so they were all set free to return home.

Jack, who was a kind boy, if you remember, gave each of them a golden feather and they went away feeling very happy for the gold would make them rich for the rest of their lives.

The King was very pleased with Jack, and since he had made the Princess not just smile but laugh out loud, he gave him half his kingdom straight away.

The Princess liked Jack too, and he could always make her smile and laugh from that day on. The golden goose feathers were sold so that all the poor old people in the kingdom could have food to eat every day. When they grew up, Jack married the Princess and they all lived happily ever after.

About the authors

Xanthe Gresham

Xanthe Gresham (pronounced "Zanthee") is a full-time storyteller. She began storytelling in 1995 and is popular with both adults and children. She has worked in the UK, Ireland, France, New Zealand, Slovenia, Holland and Switzerland. She will tell her stories almost anywhere. For example, she has had audiences in theatres, schools, museums, galleries, festivals, hospitals, community spaces, roundhouses, barges, boats, gardens, parks, woodlands and in waiting rooms!

She has worked extensively for The British Museum. She works as a storyteller for Holland Park and The Chelsea Physic Garden and is a Lecturer in Storytelling and Drama at the University of East London.

Taffy Thomas

Taffy Thomas is a leading and experienced storyteller. In the past he trained as a Literature and Drama teacher and then taught for several years. He then founded the travelling theatre and arts companies Magic Lantern, and Charivari, and then returned to concentrate on storytelling.

Taffy has a repertoire of more than 300 stories, collected mainly from oral sources. Taffy often wears his famous Tale Coat when telling stories, a beautiful embroidered coat which displays intricate images from many of the stories Taffy loves to tell.

He has appeared at arts festivals in the USA and in Norway. In 2001 he performed for the Blue Peter Prom at the Royal Albert Hall; and in 2006 was storyteller in residence at the National Centre for Storytelling in Tennessee. Taffy is currently the artistic director of Tales in Trust, the Northern Centre for Storytelling, in the Lake District. In the 2001, he was awarded an MBE for services to storytelling and charity. He tours nationally and internationally working both in entertainment and education and is also a patron of the Society for Storytelling.

Pie Corbett

Pie Corbett is an extremely well known and prominent figure in the field of education. He has worked as a primary teacher and headteacher and has also worked as an English inspector in Gloucestershire.

He edits, compiles and writes poetry books for children. He also writes resource books for teachers. He has published over 200 books. He is a selector for the 'Children's Poetry Bookshelf' and also wrote poetry objectives for the National Literacy Strategy.

In addition to his writing, Pie also runs writing workshops, runs In-service training, performs poetry and takes part in storytelling events all over the country. He has also appeared at numerous literary festivals such as those at Cheltenham, Edinburgh and Wiltshire. He is currently working with the Story Museum in Oxford as co-director of their educational outreach programme.

Jane Grell

Jane Grell was born and grew up on island of Dominica. She has been running storytelling workshops for children and adults since 1986. Now living in London, she has taken her stories to audiences around the UK. She draws heavily though not exclusively on her African-Caribbean heritage. Her storytelling thus consists of rhythm games, songs, poems, proverbs, riddles and stories.

Jane's stories have been published in various anthologies. She has worked as a writer/presenter on BBC School Radio and is a frequent contributor to Scholastic's *Literacy Time* and *Child Education*.

Hugh Lupton

Hugh Lupton became a professional storyteller in 1981. In 1985 he formed the Company of Storytellers and for twelve years the company toured Britain. Hugh has toured Africa and South America for the British Council and regularly performs in Europe and the USA. He has published several collections of folk tales.

Vivian French

Vivian was first published in 1990. Since then, she has established an enviable reputation as a writer of integrity and imagination. She has published over 200 titles, and conducts writing workshops for both children and adults, teaching at the University of the West of England and the Edinburgh College of Art.

Vivian has lived mainly in London, Bristol and now Edinburgh. She has toured from Orkney to Oklahoma, and particularly enjoyed running writing workshops in Ibiza and Majorca.

Helen East

Helen East was born in Colombo but settled in London in 1979, where she started working as a storyteller. She has directed several major regional arts and storytelling projects. Since 2002 Helen has regularly led storywalks in Shropshire and the borders. She has also led storywalks in Kew Gardens, London. She has toured South America telling stories in primary and secondary schools.

Mary Medlicott

Mary Medlicott is one of the country's leading storytellers. She works in performance, educational and community settings. Since the early 1980s she has carried out numerous residencies in schools, libraries, community centres and arts centres all over the UK. Her storytelling repertoire is formed from traditional stories from many cultures, including her native Wales.

Jess Smith

Jess Smith grew up in Scotland. As a child she lived in a bus with her parents and seven sisters travelling around the country. Jess acquired storytelling skills from her elders. Her books include *Jessie's Journey*, *Tales From the Tent*, *Tears for a Tinker* and *Bruar's Rest*.